YOU JUST DON'T WAKE UP STRONG

YOU JUST DON'T WAKE UP STRONG

TO: Victoria Litt

Peace + Blessings

Thank you for the love
+ Support !!

FABIAN THORNE

DEDICATION

I dedicate this book to my **Lord and** Saviour, family,

my church family, and **host of su**pporters."

CONTENTS

INTRODUCTION

A small child, destined to live with a life-altering disability.

A young boy, eager and willing to do anything to play football against all odds.

A budding adult with dreams and aspirations.

All these characters have led to the man that I strive to be and the man I have become.

My name is Fabian Thorne, a child of God who is positive, caring and focused. I am also an athlete, a trainer and an advocate for fitness. As a goal-driven businessman, mentor, son, husband and father, my mission is not just to inspire boys and men, but everyone who has ever had a dream, a goal, a wish, or a hunger to be a better and successful person. To everyone who has been through or is going through the trials and tribulations of life, I want to encourage you to never give up. Despite your financial or social status, there is always a way to overcome your circumstances.

"You Just Don't Wake Up Strong" is a testament to both my failures and my successes in life. From being told by doctors that I would never be able to play football, to being the number one player at Delaware State University. Despite being sent to prison for 15 months, I was able to return to society and build a fitness business from the ground up. This book outlines the ongoing progression of my business and other entities that I have incorporated into my plan.

My faith in God is my guide **for staying** on the right path. I am a true testament **to the fa**ct that not all storms come to disrupt your **life, some** come to clear your path. I wrote this book **to give you** direction and actionable advice.

As someone who has b**een through** a lot, I can provide inspiration. I might **not have** all the answers to your situation, but I enco**urage you** to believe that everything you do, good or b**ad, has a** purpose in your life.

My actions are all a part **of me and** I wish to offer you information and guidance **through** my experience.

I hope this book gives **you some** direction and focus after reading about my **life. If a**nything, I hope it puts a smile on your face **and warms** your heart.

God bless you.

CHAPTER 1

IN THE BEGINNING

My name is Fabian Lamont Thorne. I was born on February 21, 1973. I am the middle child of the three children born to my parents Billy Cefus Thorne and Annie Thorne. I have a brother, Chad, and a sister, Angela. I was born in South Hill, Virginia in a small town, with only one traffic light. In my early years, I was raised in the country. We lived in a house with a chicken coup in South Hill, before circumstances forced us to move to the city in East Orange, New Jersey.

When I was two years old, my mom became very concerned about me, as she saw that I was bumping into walls and not walking correctly. One day, she sat me on the side of the bed and took a good look at me. She looked me in the eyes and realized she could see straight through my left pupil. As any mother can imagine, being able to see straight through her child's eye scared her. In a panic, she asked my father to rush me to the hospital. My father did not react with the same concern as my mom did. Upon her request, he replied that he would not take me to the hospital. My father wasn't very loving, nor was he around much. My mom then took me to the Children's Hospital in Richmond, VA where I was rushed into surgery. The doctors saw that there was a cancerous tumor eating away at my left eye which required immediate surgery. Without surgery, the tumor could have moved to my brain, putting me in a far worse state. At that time, no effort was made to save my eye. It was simply removed, thus saving my life. God bless my mother for having the sense of urgency not to delay but to act immediately. I was then given a prosthetic eye.

When I was four years old, my mom packed up and moved us to New Jersey because there weren't that many job opportunities in South Hill, V.A. My father hadn't been supporting us and my mom knew it was time for a new start. Her brother, Eddie, was living in New Jersey so she decided to move there. We started our new life on North Munn Avenue. We still had our southern hospitality at home but being raised in a city was new to me and my siblings. The kids at the new school were brutal towards me when they noticed that something was wrong with my left eye. I couldn't hide my differences and the kids picked on me relentlessly through first and second grade. Eventually, it became too much for me to bear and I felt like lashing back in frustration. One day, I took the prosthetic eye out and chased the kids around the playground with it. The principal, a good man, took me to his office. I will never forget what he said to me. He sat me down and said "Son, your behavior will not be tolerated. You cannot do that. It is not appropriate for you to take your eye out and chase the kids around the playground". On that day I realized that I had to find a different outlet for my frustration. I was a bright child who always got good grades. This wasn't about someone who didn't understand and wanted to make trouble in school. There was something different about me and I wondered why I was going through this challenge; what I couldn't see.

Not long after this incident, my mom took me to try out for little league football. Football was something I had always loved, and always asked my mom about. In fact, my mom often said I was born with a football in my hand. She finally took me down to Oval Park in East Orange, right across the street from the playground where the school kids would pick on me. There was never any doubt that I wanted to play football and she wondered if when the time came, I would be allowed to play. She was convinced I had the drive and faith to play the game but wondered if others would see that determination despite my disability. I was six years old, a good kid, but in need of something to channel my anger. Football seemed like a great way to channel my anger.

When my mom took me to the field to sign up that year, the coach, Stanley Edwards said I was too young and needed to wait a year. I cried so much that I was almost inconsolable. I wanted to play football so badly. But I had to patiently wait all year.

The following year, I went back to the field and picked up the form for the doctor to sign and confirm my fitness to play. At the first appointment, the doctor had to test what I could see. He pointed to an eye chart and told me to cover my right eye and read for him. I looked at the doctor and told him that if I covered my right eye I wouldn't be able to see anything. Once he realized I was blind in my left eye, he refused to clear me to play football. Just like the last time, I cried. That same day, my mother took me to two more doctors, both of whom said the same thing. I could not be approved to play football.

My mom did not stop trying and continued looking for doctors. The fifth doctor we saw was Dr. Ricardi.

He examined me the same way as the others did. He noted, however, how determined my mother and I were. He could see that she was not going to give up on me. Although he knew that I couldn't see out of my left eye, he saw that I could move my head. He said I would have to wear a special face mask or goggles; something to protect my real eye and with that, he gave me the approval and signed the form. I could play! I was one of the happiest kids alive. I went back to Oval Park in East Orange and signed up to play.

I remember the first time I put my shoulder pads and helmet on. That day, someone hit me on my left side and knocked me off my feet but I wasn't discouraged. The coach came over and instead of asking "Son, are you alright?", He said "Son, listen, you have to keep your head on a swivel. You don't have the peripheral vision on the left side. You have to keep your head moving at all times." And I understood. In the game of football, that phrase is said by coaches to describe a player who needs to watch out for where the big hit might come from. I will never forget what I learned that day, that I could play this game. This game was what I needed at the age of seven. From that day on, I had an outlet to channel my energy. Any time I had some negative energy to release, I would channel it into football. I was able to release the frustration and anger I had bottled up and use it in a positive way.

Playing football allowed me to understand and accept who I was. I learned how to become a team player. I learned how to embrace my disability. As I got older, I realized that I didn't consider it a disability because I never remembered being able to see with two eyes. Having only one eye was all I knew. Every year, I got better and better at playing football.

The obstacle of learning something new increased my strength. With each year, I played different positions including inside linebacker, which allowed me to call my own plays and made me the captain of the team. On offense, I was an offensive guard and then became a star running back. I had done all of this despite my young age. I was in practice one day and I remember feeling so good that I looked up to the sky and said: "Lord I hope I'll be playing this game for a very long time". I also thanked the Lord for giving me the opportunity to play football. I never took it for granted. I was breaking records and I set the bar high for myself. It did something for me. It pulled me out of a dark closet and gave me something concrete to stand for, something that gave me value. Playing football also kept me from fighting kids in school. I was more focused on how I could get better at the game, while also focusing on my grades. I wanted to maintain my A's and B's, as I wanted to be a scholar.

Some of the things you lose in life you end up gaining elsewhere. I believe that, in losing my sight, God gave me the ability to work through problems and school work a little better than others without a disability. Those questions I had as a young child, like wondering why I was different, and being forced to face the challenges set before me, were starting to make sense. My "disability" had forced me to take the only route I could toward success, towards getting what I wanted out of life. I had to work twice as hard and have twice as much faith in myself and God as I might have had if things had been easy or "normal". I saw that I was not only ready for the challenge but capable of overcoming it. Through my challenges, I gained all the discipline I needed to move forward with my dreams. Although my dreams were inspiring, the reality of my situation was hard. One of my biggest challenges was growing up in the city of East Orange. I was surrounded by poverty. We experienced being on welfare, Medicaid, and food stamps. I remember my mom sending us to the corner store to get food. I would look around the store to see if any of my friends were there before I pulled out the food stamps. Back then it wasn't the EBT card they use now, it was paper food stamps. Paper with different color ink represented different denominations of money. I felt ashamed, but I did it so we could eat. Being on welfare created situations that would challenge you. Other people weren't on it and dealing with those moments always made me feel like changing my situation when I got old enough. Despite all these things, we were happy. My family lived in a building with four apartments. My grandmother and two aunts lived down the hall from us. My uncles came and went, but women were always around. I never had a stable male figure in my life, so all the women supported me in everything that I did, including football.

We lived above a fish market, corner store, laundromat, and cleaners. My aunt would sweep the sidewalk out front as if she owned the building. We took care of our surroundings and lived as one big family. If we didn't have food, we went down the hall to each other's apartments to eat. We pooled our money and resources for birthdays and holidays and enjoyed great meals together. For birthdays we might get one gift, presented by the entire family. My mom baked the cakes from scratch and we appreciated it. All of it.

Those years from elementary school through middle school were years filled with love and comfort because I was surrounded by many friends and family. That love and support got me through the challenging times and helped me face going to high school.

As I grew older, I knew that once I got to high school my life goals would be set. Although I wanted to be a football player, I also wanted to be an entrepreneur. One of my goals was to buy my mom a house and a car from the proceeds of my success. I remember telling myself when I got my driver's license that I would maintain a good record. I watched my friends drive without licenses, not caring about the potential consequences. I didn't want to do that. I was surrounded by moral values that were instilled in me by my extended family. For me, going into high school gave me the opportunity to do something special and I knew that successfully completing high school would bring me that much further to living a life that incorporated those values.

As a freshman, I got an opportunity to play varsity football. I was the only freshman on the team, which was, at the time, unprecedented. This was another challenging experience as one of the coaches made it tough for me. He encouraged the upperclassmen to make it tough for me in an attempt to make me quit. I will never forget those practices. Coach West had one of his best players attack me during drills and when that didn't work he tried again with another senior player. He was clearly upset that his tactics weren't working. He eventually learned that I wasn't a quitter.

I had been fighting all my life. As with all challenges in my life, I fought through and overcame.

During my freshman year, I started as an outside linebacker, making defensive plays in the game. My other coach and mentor during that time was Tony Pierce. I met him in the park one day during my last year of middle school and he invited me to practice with the varsity team. I made the team that year and went on to become a leader and a captain. Although Coach Pierce left my senior year of high school we kept in touch and he continued to be my mentor.

In my sophomore year, Coach Pierce took me to a youth rally and encouraged me to speak that night. I was surprised and unprepared, but he gave me cue cards to speak from. The main speaker at the rally was the great Reggie White. At that time, Reggie White was a professional football player who eventually became a legend. He was also a God-fearing man. He taught me that I could use my words to inspire others and that the words I shared should also be the words I lived by. That night, I spoke first and the youth in attendance treated me like I was a celebrity. They even asked for my autograph. I was proud of myself as I was on the podium, sharing a stage with a legend. Coach Pierce also introduced me to the organization Fellowship Christians and Athletes (FCA). Their organization is geared toward reaching out to the youth.

Though I was young, I knew I had God in my life. My relationship with God helped me through all my challenges. God has been in my corner. He has protected me and has kept me safe. He has given me the desire to be greater than what I could imagine. Still, God won't give you more than you can handle.

He knows best, and you have **to trust** the process and have faith. I knew what was **happening** in my life was orchestrated and governed **by God.** When faced with obstacles, God taught me **and made** me feel like I could do anything. The football field **w**as the platform where He taught me those **lessons.** At times, it was like David and Goliath on the **field. D**avid, an Israelite from the first book of Samue**l in the Ol**d Testament in the Bible, battles the Philist**ine giant,** Goliath. David kills Goliath with just a ston**e and his** sling. It teaches us a lesson about facing giant **problems** or impossible situations. I was a mere five **feet seve**n inches and I had a muscular build. I was **playing** with guys who were over six feet tall, but **I never fe**lt like I didn't belong. I remember when I w**ent on to** college, I said to myself "All of this is so new **but I'm rea**dy. What's next Lord?". Every time I played **football at** a higher level,

I wondered where I would go next. What encounters awaited me next? I was learning so much through my involvement in football. One thing I however had to learn, was how to overcome injuries.

It was my senior year of high school. Our first game of the season and we were playing against Seton Hall Prep High School. In one of the plays, I was running with the ball down the sideline. The opposition knew that if he attempted to tackle me high or jump on me, I would take him for a ride into the end zone and score. Instead, he decided to take my knee out. That tackle took me out for the rest of the game. The injury sent me to Columbus Hospital. I was sent home with a sprain and was out for four games and never had proper rehabilitation. One thing I had to learn was how to deal with and overcome injury. I never knew exactly what was wrong with my knee. It often gave out on me while I was playing. I began to doubt whether I would be able to play football past high school, but Coach Pierce suggested that I go to Trinity College, a Christian University, in Deerfield, Illinois. It was there that I met another great mentor, Coach Leslie Frazier. He played for the Chicago Bears in the 1985 Super bowl. He was also the head coach of the Minnesota Vikings and he coached with the Philadelphia Eagles and the Cincinnati Bengals. He was also on the coaching staff of the Tampa Bay Buccaneers as a defensive coach in Florida. Currently, he is a defensive coordinator for the Buffalo Bills. He has certainly put in his time with the NFL and he is still a friend and mentor to this day.

While I was at Trinity College, I learned how to apply myself better to my school work and football. The coach saw me running in practice one day and he noticed that something was wrong with my knee. He said, "Son, you look good, but you have something wrong with your knee". He sent me to a sports doctor in Chicago to have it checked out. I was told that I had a partially torn anterior cruciate ligament (commonly known as the ACL) and cartilage damage. This type of injury occurs from a twisting action where the foot is planted in the ground or from landing from a jump and the knee turns excessively inwards. All this time, I had been running around on my knee not knowing what was wrong. It was nice to finally have a diagnosis. While in Chicago, I had surgery and rehabilitated my knee. At that time, I felt it was time for me to get closer to home so I transferred to Delaware State University (DSU). Coach Frazier gave me a great letter of recommendation and I transferred. Another obstacle confronted me at this time.

In colleges and universities that have sports programs, there are two associations that determine divisions for the athletic levels. The most widely known is the National Collegiate Athletic Association (NCAA) and the other one is the National Association of Intercollegiate Athletics (NAIA). The NCAA has 3 divisions with level one being the highest, based on their guidelines for a college's number of teams, team size, game calendar and financial support. The NAIA is made up of smaller 4-year colleges with 2 divisions.

Trinity College is an NAIA division 2 college and DSU is an NCAA division 1 school. Because of a proposition enacted in 1986 by the NCAA, I was not able to play football for one year. The proposition, called Proposition 48 is a regulation that stipulates minimum high school grades and standardized test scores that student- athletes must meet to participate in college athletic competition. It also says that the athlete must have the successful completion of 16 core courses.

It was during the spring of 1993 that I transferred to DSU. I wanted to play but I had no essential video footage of my performance to give to the coach. All I had was a letter of recommendation from my former coach. I sat in the Delaware State Football office with Coach Bill Collick, who told me to go home and see how much money I could come back with. I went home and came back with thirty dollars. I said, "Coach, this is all I got". My mom worked hard to make ends meet. She did her best to send me a twenty-five dollar check every other month. But I knew I could play. I said, "Coach, if you give me the opportunity to get into this school I will keep my grades up so that I can play the game". Thankfully, he accepted me into the school. He took me to the financial aid and admissions office and I was able to get financial aid. The football team covered whatever else I needed toward my education. During that spring, I got out on the field to practice and I quickly made a name for myself. The coaches were impressed with me, but I still had to wait to play because of the regulations. I had maintained a 3.3 grade point average (GPA). In the fall of 1993, I still could not play. The coach allowed me to practice on full-contact days, which means the players would practice in full safety gear, helmets, and uniform. As I was not supposed to be playing in games, I was not assigned all my equipment, so I used my high school helmet during practices.

Three months after transferring to Delaware State I learned a valuable lesson. My friends and I were at a local sports bar having a good time, shooting pool and listening to music. Suddenly, a fight broke out. Some of my teammates and colleagues were fighting with the locals. I was at the pool table with three of my female friends. My first instinct was to make sure those friends got out. As we were rushing and running out of the bar, a cop told me to stop running but I kept running. As I got outside, I came upon another cop that had a police dog with him. He used pepper spray on me while I was running. Everything became very blurry, but I kept running hysterically in the parking lot. I saw a young lady sitting in her truck and tried to get in with her but she locked the doors and wouldn't allow me in. By this time the pepper spray had set in, so I just laid on the ground. The officer came up to me, turned me over and continued to spray the pepper spray in my face. The ladies that were playing pool with me were crying and yelling at him to stop, that I was blind in one eye. After he heard that, he stopped, then handcuffed me and put me in the police car and took me to jail. I ended up on the front page of the local newspaper. The article said the football player was in a bar fight and was incarcerated. I went to my coach and explained what happened to him. He had just given me an opportunity to stay in college and already I was being displayed negatively in the paper. The President of the university wanted to kick me out but my coach went to intercede for me and asked him to give me another chance. My coach believed in me so much that he jeopardized his job to convince the President of our school to allow me to stay. I will forever be grateful for that. I went on to prove to him that I wasn't a troublemaker. I showed him that I could capitalize on the opportunity, but most importantly, I developed a relationship with him and he remains my mentor and friend till today. That relationship helped me navigate through college.

Once again, you just don't wake up strong. Those trials in my life made me what I am today. I had to go through something to make it to where I am now.

On full contact days, I was on scout team offense, the practice squad consisting of freshmen and walk-ons and I went against the first team defense (the best players). I will never forget running up against guys who were very good. I thought if I played against those guys it would make us all better. For me, it was an opportunity to get better. It was an opportunity to show the coaches that I was willing to do whatever it took to prepare myself for my time. I went out with the guys and practiced day in and day out. When my time came in 1994, I was behind a fifth-year senior. Three games into the season he wasn't getting the job done the way the coaches wanted him to. Eventually, they started me in the Florida Bethune-Cookman game. Unfortunately, I made a mistake that day. During a play, someone blindsided me on my left side. I fumbled (dropped) the ball and put our defense in a bad situation because they were on the 12-yard line and they yielded to a field goal. Upset with my mistake, I tried to hide from Coach Collick on my way to the sideline, but he called me and told me that if I put the ball on the carpet (turf) one more time I would walk back to Dover, Delaware from Florida. I went back out and finished the game with three touchdowns, 165 yards and ESPN (Entertainment and Sports Programming Network) player of the week. I broke a 69-yard run for a touchdown. I took over that starting fullback position and I never looked back. I ended up finishing the 1994 season with 1,089 yards and 13 touchdowns, which made me a pre-season All American for the upcoming 1995 season.

CHAPTER 2

ALL EYES ON ME

The year 1995 marked my last season as a Delaware State University Hornet. With lots of expectations upon me, I could no longer sneak up on my opponents. So, I prepared myself by training harder and smarter during the summer before the start of the 1995 football season. One of my goals was to gain more yards than I did in the previous year. The 1995 season was very challenging, but all the hard work eventually paid off. I ended my senior season with 1,296 yards and 12 touchdowns, thus putting me in the running for the rushing title for entire Mid-Eastern Athletic Conference (MEAC). Ultimately, I came up three yards short for the rushing title.

The following year, 1996 involved me continuing my education after playing football. I believed I would get an opportunity to play in the NFL, and in March that year, a particular NFL team offered me a mini-camp contract. The contract was however never fulfilled because I believe they became aware of my disability and decided to back out of the deal. Nevertheless, the phone call that I got from that team inspired and encourage me to keep pushing. This was when I met my first trainer, Larry Athill, through my agent. He helped me with my speed and agility, trying to prepare me for football combines and private workouts.

That year, I got married and having a wife motivated me even more to keep striving for my dream of becoming a professional football player. Being very young, it was tough in the beginning. I was the running back coach for DSU. At the same time, I was training and trying to get to the next level.

Eventually, it became too much of a financial burden to stay in Delaware, so my wife and I had to move to New Jersey in 1998. We stayed with my family, at my mother's house along with my sister and her husband, my brother and my uncle. This was meant to be a pit stop for us. My wife and I slept on the floor and before we knew it, my wife was pregnant with my son. I was on my grind, working jobs and still training and trying to make ends meet. Knowing that my wife was pregnant, I had to find a full-time job to support my family. I started a job as a floor counselor at an adult halfway house. That job enabled us to get a place of our own. We moved into a one-bedroom apartment above a salon in East Orange, New Jersey that was and is still owned by a long-time friend of the family. We lived there for a short period of time. It was still a challenging time financially, trying to stay with a steady job. I eventually left my job at the halfway house because I witnessed a system that was failing. They treated the adults unfairly and did not give them the opportunity to be successful in society. I couldn't stand to see that, so I went to work for the company Price Waterhouse Coopers, as a document imaging specialist in Totowa, New Jersey. That still wasn't enough as I wasn't fed spiritually, and I was yearning to play football. I was still training and trying to make a better opportunity. That job just wasn't fulfilling. I felt miserable because I didn't have the passion to excel at that type of job.

My heart was on football and being an entrepreneur, but knowing I had a family at home, I had to do what I had to do. That company ended up down-sizing, so I left that job and found something different, cleaning hospitals. I never had the problem of getting a job and swallowing my pride to do something I really didn't want to do, so I cleaned the hospitals to make a way for my family. I was watching my young son grow and it encouraged me. I will never forget when he was born, 4 years into our marriage on December 2, 2000. Fabian Amani Thorne. We call him LB for "little bear". He was my inspiration and I kept pushing and kept driving to change my situation so I could find true happiness. A few years into my son's life, despite my effort, the financial burden took a toll on our marriage. We decided to separate.

A few weeks after our separation, I received a call from my cousin and he told me about an open tryout in Petersburg, Virginia for a professional European football league. I had still been training even though I had been going through my storm. Exercise has always been a part of me that would guide me and keep me focused and help me cope with my emotional pain and stress. I went down to Petersburg and tried out for the football league. There were about 30 guys at the tryout. It was very cold, and the tryout was outside. Out of the 30 guys, they chose two of us and I thank God for being one of those two that they chose to represent the league. Before I went to the tryout, my wife called me saying she was at the hospital with **our son.** She said he had a seizure. He was 2 years **old at the** time. I called my pastor and she talked to **me and** encouraged me because I wasn't sure what **to do when** I was all the way in Virginia. She reminded me that the enemy will always try to discourage you. She also said I was there for a reason, that **I should** do what I went there to do and come on **home. It** made sense to me because I was so far **away. The** doctors didn't have an answer as to why **my son had** the seizures. He only had one or two **more seizures** and never had them again. I ended up **having m**y son for that weekend after I came back **from Virginia** and I got to spend some quality time **with him.** This was very important to me because **my dad** was not in my life, so I promised my son **I would** always be there for him. It was not a good feeling growing up and I never wanted my son to experience that.

A few months later in May of 2003, I headed overseas to play football for the Erding Bulls in Erding, Germany. My experience in Germany was enlightening and fulfilling. Not only was it a beautiful place, but I learned a lot about nutrition. The food there was prepared differently. They did not inject meats and poultry with preservatives, nor did they use pesticides on the fruits, vegetables and other crops. It was a very healthy way of living and it was thrilling to know that this was how food should taste and fuel your body the right way. That experience opened my mind to the differences between their country and ours. I believe that the nutrition regimen I was exposed to while in Germany enabled me to perform at a high level. I led the league in rushing yards and touchdowns. It gave me a great sense of accomplishment. This whole experience was refreshing to my mind and spirit because I was still going through my separation. Any money I made, I sent back home. The opportunity to experience a different culture facilitated a new beginning for me, which allowed me to come back home and find a way to build my brand.

Upon my return home, I was eager to begin my career as a football player and an entrepreneur. I was hopeful that I could work things out in my marriage, but that didn't happen. My wife was fed up with the whole situation and tired of dealing with all our issues. So, in December of 2003, right after Christmas and in a day I will never forget, my wife moved back to her hometown, New Haven, Connecticut. I understood it, I really did, but the distressing thing was that my son was leaving too. I wasn't angry at her, at all. I was sad because of the type of person I had become and how hard I had tried to make things work. I always strived to be a better father, so it really hurt me to see my son leave. However, that experience did something for me, it made me grow up. It made me realize that this little boy didn't ask to be here. I will never forget that moment when I looked into his eyes and I hugged him and kissed him. He was three years old when he left, and I cried like a baby because I felt like a part of my soul was being ripped out. But then again, I wasn't angry at her because she had to do what was necessary to get back on her feet. In the process of it, I made sure that we could co-parent amicably to ensure that our son was raised by both of us.

So, with her moving back to Connecticut, I moved back in with my mother, trying to start all over, which was frustrating. At that time, she was in a 2-bedroom apartment, living with her brother. I thought to myself, look at what my life has become. I had to dig deep and find a way to get out of the rut I had gotten myself into and get myself back on track. The ministry I attended and still attend to this day, Jehovah's Circle, started my movement forward. The foundation and backbone of Jehovah's Circle helped me find my way and get back on my feet. Nevertheless, some time passed, and I didn't want to stay in New Jersey anymore. I packed up and moved down to Virginia where I started looking for jobs because it seemed like a place where I could get ahead. I started in the real estate and mortgage business and things seemed to be going well. I was brand new to the business and I learned a lot about being a loan officer and how to do all the paperwork and how loans worked. I wasn't at the company for very long before another roadblock came into my life. I branched off from the company I was working for and went to work with someone who had mentored me through the process of learning the mortgage business. He started his own company.

I worked for him, believing that I was doing things the right way, and everything was legitimate. The girlfriend I was dating at the time worked with us at the previous job and she ended up going to this company with me. In July of 2006, my girlfriend and I got married. At the time of our marriage, the company we worked for was deteriorating. In a matter of time, his company came under investigation by the FBI, as well as all of the employees which included my wife and I.

We were under the impression that the paperwork done by us was correct, so the paper trail led to us. At this time in 2005 and continuing through 2008, the housing and banking markets across the country faced a crisis. Foreclosure would end up being at an all-time high. Homeowners across the country were dealing with losing their homes because they were placed in balloon mortgages. They had no idea how they worked and in two years, their mortgage payment would at least double to a figure they couldn't afford. They called it predatory lending. The investigation concluded with my new wife and I being charged with conspiracy to commit wire fraud. We both believed and knew we were not wrong because we had educated people on how to avoid losing their homes not helping them lose it.

Ultimately, we ended up going to prison. In the process before our incarceration, we lost our own house, so we had to pack up and move to New Jersey. For me, it was *Deja vu*, trying to start all over again. We moved on February 7th, 2007. The investigation was still ongoing at that time, so it was difficult to be in New Jersey and try to make a living with the idea of prison hanging over our heads. We were having issues and problems in our marriage because of the stress of the whole situation. Eventually, we were charged in 2008 and sentenced to federal prison. In August of 2008, I had to drive my wife to prison, as her surrender date was earlier than mine. Dropping her off was one of the most painful things I'd ever had to do. You can't imagine dropping off your wife, watching her get in a van and place her hand on the window as they drive her into the prison to say goodbye to you. It was one of the worst things ever that could rip a hole in you. As I was driving back home, so many things were going through my mind. I reached out to the judge to see if he would give me the opportunity to go visit my wife before I had to turn myself in. God gave me favor and they allowed me to go visit her. I went to visit her, and it was a very emotional visit. This woman had never experienced dealing with law enforcement this way. It just wasn't in her DNA to be in prison. Even though it was more like a camp at the facility in West Virginia with open space and access to being outside every day, it was still prison.

On my way back home from West Virginia to New Jersey, the Lord spoke to me and told me to fast before I went in. It was a Thursday; I will never forget it. That Friday I woke up and had only water for breakfast, lunch, and dinner. I cried out to the Lord asking why I had to go to the facility where I was assigned. I was supposed to be at a camp-type facility as well, but I ended up going to the Metropolitan Detention Center (MDC), a high-rise unit in Brooklyn, NY. But, I felt good getting off my face because I knew that once I fasted, I was going where I needed to be. I just needed to find out why. What was there for me? The worst thing still troubling me was having to leave my son whom I had just spent the summer with. I dreaded having to drive him back to his home in Connecticut. He was only 7 years old at the time, so I explained to him that I had to go away for a little while, but we could write to each other. That was very emotional for me as well.

The day finally came for me to self-surrender. My friend, my sister and my mother drove me to the facility. During the car ride, I was making jokes to lighten the mood because my mother and my sister were crying, very emotionally. It was just another test and obstacle that I had to go through. We got to the facility and they dropped me off and it seemed as though another part was ripped out of me. I thanked God because I knew he had me going there for a reason and I just focused on what His reason was. All these obstacles and tests made me who I was. I was going to have to reach deep within myself to discover the things that would give me strength and motivation to keep going. It was the people who loved me, those who had been by my side and those who had been there for me that made a difference in my life.

The day I walked in that prison I said, "Okay Lord, here we go". I looked right away to figure out why I was there. I was sentenced to 24 months in prison. By the grace of God, I had a woman from my public defender's office helping me. She said that I didn't deserve to go to prison and made me a promise to get me out.

Three or four months into my stay there, an opportunity presented itself. One of my colleagues was working there at the facility. He called me by my nickname, Bear, and asked me to come to his office. When he asked what I was doing there, I broke down all the details for him and he told me he was going to try to get me a job in education. That was when my eyes started to open up. What were the chances I would meet someone I went to college with and they would know me and my character and what I was about? He gave me the opportunity to **work in ed**ucation. I took an entrepreneur class called **Worksho**p in Business Opportunities (WIBO). Th**rough this**, my mind got stronger. I had a lot of time **for praying**, reading and writing. I structured my m**ain business** plan around fitness because the Lord told **me to go** with fitness. I ended up with four business **plans: fitn**ess, real estate, my clothing line and a storage **company**. I already had the name for my fitness com**pany; Buil**t2Last Fitness. I was able to teach a fitness c**lass while** I was there. In a place like this, you never k**now who** you are going to meet. I met a man that be**came my** mentor. He was an attorney and a very spiri**tual man.** We met through the education program and **we bega**n to bond and talk. He helped me write m**y infrastr**ucture for my business. He was a man of **his word** and to this day, he is still my mentor. He h**as given** me legal advice when needed. You just never know who you are going to meet.

I will never forget when I got called to the office. They told me I was getting an immediate release in 2 days, which was 2 days before Christmas Eve. I had been there almost 15 months. While I was there, I received mail saying that I was released from a civil suit that was related to our case. I found out that the Feds (FBI) found some paper trail showing that we were not trying to do anything wrong, but that was nobody but God touching the right hearts.

My immediate release was on Christmas Eve in 2009. My pastor, her husband, and her son came to pick me up because they would not allow my wife to come get me. She had already been released in

September of that year. As I was walking out of the prison, one of the correction officers said to me, "They don't release people on Christmas Eve". And I said, "The God I serve can do the impossible". He replied, "I know that's right!". I got in the van with my pastor and her family and it was just an awesome feeling. They took me to reunite with my wife and the embrace was nothing but tears of joy. Having not seen each other for well over a year and only communicating through letters brought us closer together.

My mother and family didn't know I was coming home. We kept it a secret. My wife took me to the IHOP where they were eating. I got out and walked into the restaurant. My mother screamed, cried and almost fainted. My sister screamed and cried. The people in the restaurant had no idea what was going on with all the commotion. It was an amazing feeling. It was a memory, a moment that you capture forever.

I put my plan in motion January of 2010. That month, as I began the process of getting my brand kicked off, my wife let me know she was pregnant. Hearing the news ignited my drive to work harder. I went in and started working for a fitness training company that did personal training. We were contracted to work inside a gym. I began my fitness brand and doing what God had for me to do in becoming an entrepreneur and starting my business. At that time, I started building my website. Even though I was working for someone, I was working for myself too. I knew that was only a stepping stone to start somewhere. I worked hard and started to build my clientele base and Fabian Thorne

Built2Last was born. I used the gym as a platform to continue building my brand.

Our daughter, Jayda Monae Thorne, was born on September 20, 2010. She was born with a loving, happy spirit that inspired me to never give up. She is a spitting image of me and her brother, especially in her personality and energy. My wife calls us triplets. My bloodline is the heart and depth of my soul. They are the reason why I grind so hard.

Before I knew it, it was 2011. I continued to grow my brand, did a training at one of the largest boot camps in New Jersey with 54 people. During that summer, I was forced out of the gym because I was doing my own thing and my business was growing. I saw it as an opportunity that the Lord gave me to go out on my own, so I took that leap. In taking that leap, I knew I had to secure my business and create some stability within the brand. I looked for ways to expand my business. In the past, I did motivational speaking and I wanted to implement that as well at boot camps, one-on-one training and high school football combines, all as a mobile service. I did my first high school combine in 2013 in my hometown.

With each year, my business grew, and I had done different events for different organizations. One of the greatest organizations I had worked with was FP Youth Outcry who host their own Healthy Olympics for the city of Newark. Al-Tariq Best, the CEO and founder of this organization was a childhood friend of mine. I am grateful for him and the opportunity his organization provided for me. He brought me in for 3 years to do the healthy Olympics. We focused on all wards of Newark and prepared the kids with exercise in preparation for each event. I also did a boot camp for a company called Lycored. They started a new campaign within their company to promote employee health and fitness. I did motivational speaking for numerous high schools, including Dover High School in Delaware. I also did a football combine for Dover High School, which was one of my most successful. All of this was part of the plan that God gave me. He also gave me the ultimate part of the business, which was to build my private training facility.

Today, we are still doing things to bring the brand to a new level in fitness and expanding it with a different type of training. Sports training is my niche market. I focus on sports training, high school athletes, little league and multiple sports, not just football.

CHAPTER 3

FINDING MY PURPOSE

Growing up, my mother raised us in the church. We would pray and read Bible stories at home. Every Sunday my mom would make us get up, eat breakfast and get dressed for church. I would hide my church shoes, thinking it would get me out of having to go but that didn't work. Going to Bible study on Sunday mornings wasn't fun for me. I wanted to be somewhere playing football. Although I didn't care to go, I always learned a valuable lesson.

Church gave me a foundation to build upon. I realized that the experience wasn't about the church or the people, it was about having a relationship with God. It became more apparent that our spirit man makes us who we are.

The different challenges in my life, such as the complete loss of vision in my left eye started to give me a sense of who I was. God blessed me to be able to play one of the most violent and aggressive sports in the world. Playing football was the start of me connecting spiritually with God. I noticed that my vision on the football field would guide me through the trials and tribulations that I faced off the field as well. Being able to run through opposing players as if I had super vision further let me know that I wasn't running alone. My extensive success in the sport let me know that God was with me and guided me through it all.

This power to recognize what God was displaying within me continued to grow stronger. I knew that I had to keep my spiritual foundation balanced through prayer and communing with God. In life, you will be challenged. That's what causes growth. One of the mottos that I live by is "It's not *what* you go through, it's *how* you go through that determines the type of person you will become".

My relationship with God was the reason that I began to understand my purpose for living. At some point, the Pentecostal church we were raised in started to become more governed by the laws and rules of man. I then started to shy away from that type of environment. Once again, knowing God for myself kept me from having any resentment towards the church. Knowing how God has opened my heart, by feeling and seeing His glory, gave me a new sense of being spiritually tuned in, which I credit to my leader, my pastor, who is a true woman of God. I am in a ministry that is led by His Spirit which has allowed me to find my purpose. One day in a church service, as God was speaking through my leader, He said that I had a kingdom inside of me. I knew hearing this from Him that I needed to find time to seek Him for revelation. The thing about God is, He doesn't always reveal things to you the way you want Him to, but that is what makes Him God.

During this time, I was working, training clients at the gym and doing motivational speaking to inspire others. I began to receive phone calls, text messages and comments on social media from people I didn't know. They relayed to me how inspiring and motivating I was for them. It was through this that I built my brand, Fabian Thorne Built2Last. It became apparent to me that the kingdom inside of me was the people that I had positively affected and would continue to help in my journey. I'd truly found my purpose. I thank the Lord for placing that kingdom inside of me.

My story did not always smell like roses, yet through the "thornes" that have wounded me so deeply, I was able to re-develop myself, heal my soul and come back bigger, better, stronger and share my motivation from within to inspire others.

Sometimes, we truly have to hit rock bottom to be able to discover what we were actually put on this earth for. The best time to find your strength is when you are challenged with the unknown, the unexplained, and the very essence of all that you do not understand. My faith and trust in God allowed me to maintain and move forward. God allowed me to understand what I would be pursuing when I got out of prison. It was in prison that I truly found my purpose. There is no better way to explain the power from within than in the journal that follows.

I would like to share with you, heartfelt words from my journal that helped me get through one of the most challenging times in my life. This journal consists of words written to my son and conversations he and I had during that time.

Prison Journal

August 12, 2008 - I sit down with my son to explain that daddy has to go off to prison on September 9, 2008. This is one of the hardest things to tell my seven-year-old child. It is every bit of an emotional outcry that somehow makes both of us more attached to each other. My son is very inquisitive about how and why this is happening to his dad who, in his eyes, is the greatest dad in the world and who cannot be a bad person. My son is very mature for his age, so I have to explain to him that sometimes it's not you who is bad, but the people that you deal with who are. I make sure that he understands that it's very important to choose your friends wisely.

August 17, 2008 – It's time to take my son back home to his mother in Connecticut. Once again, I have to prepare myself for another emotional roller coaster ride. I do all I can that day to tire my son out, so he will sleep the whole 2-hour trip home. It works for most of the ride. The first half hour is very emotional for both of us. I'm relieved but still sad when he falls asleep. Looking in my rearview mirror at my precious little boy sleeping like an angel makes me realize how important it is for me to go do what I need to do so I can get back to him. The love that we share can never be broken and I vow to him to never ever leave him like this again!

September 9, 2008 – My mom, sister, one of my best friends and I drive to MDC, Brooklyn so I can self-surrender. My family members, who are very emotional people, take me on another emotional roller coaster ride. On the way to prison, I have to be strong so that my family will be alright. I know that it is one of the toughest things for my mother and sister to drop me off at the prison as I've never been incarcerated to do any extended time.

Meanwhile, I get accustomed to prison life and I find myself missing my son more and more every day because I realize that I won't be seeing him every weekend like I am used to doing.

September 11, 2008 – I finally leave the medical intake unit and go to my living quarters. Unit 53 cell is a lower level cell.

September 12, 2008 – Finally I get a chance to use the phone to call home and call my son. The first thing my son says to me is "Dad, I love you, are you okay? Anybody messing with you? Dad, I'm doing good in school!". All the things a proud dad would love to hear. As the days pass and Halloween is approaching, my son is once again excited about who he wants to be for Halloween. Dad must not get emotional because I realize that I won't be there with him for the first time in seven years. It's hard to swallow but I do it to avoid an outcry. It's a love that is indescribable! Another month is gone and I have to focus on preparing myself for another family-oriented holiday.

November 9, 2008 – I'm 2 months into this prison bid and I'm finding myself getting a bit challenged, spiritually. So, I take time out each day to lay out on my cell floor and weep and pray for God's guidance, peace of mind and a calm spirit to endure this obstacle I'm facing. It works for a couple of weeks as I feel myself getting stronger spiritually, physically and getting closer to understanding my purpose for coming through this experience. As I use the energy from missing my son each day, it helps the time to pass.

November 22, 2008 – My emotions are beginning to surface as Thanksgiving arrives. It's a joyous occasion for our family every year. We all prepare food or contribute in some way, whether it is cleaning up, going food shopping, carrying groceries, or leading the family prayer before dinner is served. For me, it's been a little bit of everything other than cooking. One of the most important moments for me has been watching my son grow each year and evolving to be more and more just like his dad. As he plays with all his cousins, having fun without a care in the world, he always stops what he is doing and comes and tells me how much he loves me. Giving me the hug of my life, that sends chills up my spine and runs wild through my veins.

Thanksgiving Day – I call home and the family is doing what they always do, enjoying themselves. My son gets on the phone with sheer excitement. 'Hey dad, I love you, dad, I miss you dad and please come home'. My reply to his words of affirmation and concern, that touched the depth of my soul, "I love you, son, you are the best son in the world and dad is doing good because you motivate me every minute of the day. Yes, I will be home soon, my son". Saying I will see you later is better than goodbye. As I hang up the phone, I quickly return to my cell to release the pain and hurt from being away from him like this. The help from reading my Bible, praying and shedding tears, puts me back in focus on doing this time and not letting the time do me. The next day, I'm back to working out and concentrating on completing one of my business plans.

December 2, 2008 – I call my son to say happy birthday to him and see if he received the birthday card that I made for him. Fabian Amani Thorne, born December 2, 2000, is now eight years old and daddy can only speak to him on the phone. It hurts but I refuse to spoil his special day by being selfish because I'm not with him. All I want is for my son to be happy and loved by everyone on his special day. I constantly tell myself I will never allow this to happen again. My job is to nurture him, love him, discipline him, provide for him, protect him and most of all, raise him in a God-fearing home. I will not let my son be fatherless like I was.

December 24, 2008 – Christmas Eve and these special occasions keep rolling in one after the next. My son deserves gifts for Christmas, as well as his birthday, so I make arrangements with his mother and my family to make sure he gets all his gifts. Everything works out as planned and I'm happy and most of all, he is happy for what daddy has done for him. It means the world to me to make sure my son is well taken care of. I'm getting reports that my son is doing well in school so far. I speak to my son at least twice a week and I always make sure he knows how important it is to pay attention to his teachers. "You have to listen, so you can learn what is being taught to you."

January 1, 2009 – Its New Year's Day I reach out to my son and my family to say Happy New Year. Once again, I encourage him to stay focused on his school work and also not forget to do his push-ups and sit-ups, which he has been doing since the age of 4. From time to time, I have to remind him to make sure he is eating his vegetables, so he can be strong like his dad.

February 21, 2009 – I call home today to hear my son tell me happy birthday. My son sends me a hand-made card that takes me back on another emotional roller coaster. This time it is a bit too much because the tears will not stop falling down my face. Thank God I am alone in my cell.

March 15, 2009 – Okay, I've made it through that hurdle and I'm so grateful for the love that God has placed in my life for my son and his mother. My son is having a difficult time dealing with his dad being in prison. He is causing problems in school with his peers and disrupting the class. The teacher is calling for a conference with his parents, so we can resolve the problem. My son explains to his mom that he is angry because he wants his dad. So, it's time to enforce the values that I taught my son about respect, perseverance and the fear of God. I talk to him with sternness and conviction, so he can understand the seriousness of his actions. During the conversation, I can feel that he is upset with himself for disappointing me and himself. I firmly let him know it's okay to feel hurt about where I am, but he must find positive ways to release that feeling. If he does that, he will begin to mature that much sooner. I let him know that I love him, and I expect good things from him. He stops crying and tells me that he is sorry, and he loves me forever and until infinity. For the next 45 days, everything is back to normal with my son. Every other day, I call him and let him know that daddy is doing okay.

April 3, 2009 – I've been working in the library for almost 3 days now and I can't quite keep myself together emotionally. Its 8 months and I still haven't seen my son yet and I feel like giving up, but I can't because if I do, I'm no good for my son, who looks up to me and most of all who needs me. So, I shake it off until I get back to the unit and call my son to make sure he is okay. The phone call gives me renewed life to keep pushing forward. I have never had my freedom taken away from me, and to top it off, placed inside of a high-rise building where I can't get any sunlight. It's a very mentally and emotionally challenging experience. One thing is for sure, either it makes you better or makes you worse, there is no in-between. Fall or rise, it's all up to your will to win. My strength comes from knowing that God is my source.

Okay, it's May now, and I call my son only to hear how upset his mom is because she is frustrated with trying to get him to act right. So, I listen to her vent and as she finishes venting, she says that our son needs to be on medication. I pause to make sure I respond in a respectful fashion. I plead with her and I ask her if she can hold out on giving him any medication until I get home. He only has 45 days left to do in school and I should be home. She says that she will wait, but to be honest with you, I truly don't know if she will or not because I'm still incarcerated.

As the month of May ends and we come into June 2009, I become very emotional some days because the visions of my son on medication are heavy on my heart and mind. I need to express it to someone that can feel my pain, so I do. My boss allows me to vent my frustration about my son's mother's inability to see the damage medication would cause our son. After venting to my 2 supervisors it helps me to be strong and prayerful as well as elevate my faith in God.

June 20, 2009 – The end of the school year arrives and my son is asking me if I will be home, so he can spend the summer with me as usual. I tell him that's the plan but it's really up to the courts to file my reduction. His mother tells me that my son has to take a reading class that costs $160.00 every 2 weeks and she also signed him up for basketball camp. I make sure that I contribute to the cost for my son's reading class and basketball camp as best I can. I wish I can be there to help my son with his reading and teach him how to play basketball, just like we were doing before I came to prison. So, I do my best to encourage him and give him some advice when playing basketball.

July 2009 – July is here, and my son is now ready to play football, but daddy is still in prison. This is the only time I feel like I will not let his mother sign him up for football. It may sound a bit selfish on my part, but she can't prepare him for this sport nor can any male friend of hers. Football is the essence of my true nature and it won't be compromised by anyone. My son deserves the opportunity to embrace this special moment with his dad who respects and loves the game of football for what it has done and can do for my son. The game of football is a parallel to life. I want to be there to give my son every opportunity to grow as a man through this wonderful sport. I, as his Father, owe him and the sport everything I have, to give my son and myself the opportunity to continue to become the best that a man can be.

August 2009 – My son is anxious and curious to know when his dad is coming home. All I can do is encourage him by telling him I will be home very soon. He responds by asking me if I need him to come to the jail and tell the policeman to let me go. I laugh a little because I know he really would do it if he could and it shows me how much he loves his dad. So deep down inside I'm hurting because he needs me, and I need him but, I laugh to keep him encouraged.

August 27, 2009 – It's the first day of school and my son can't go because his mother can't find his birth certificate, something she never loses. A week before school my mom orders a birth certificate for my son and mailed it to his mother. So, he starts school on August 28, 2009, which is not bad.

September 2009 – My son tells me he is doing good in school, and sends me a letter with his test score (108) because he did the bonus. He also drew 3 football helmets, the Pittsburg Steelers, the NY Giants (which is his team) and the Dallas Cowboys which is my team and he ends the letter with, "P.s. the best dad in the world". It always makes me feel special because I know in my heart and soul that he truly means it. Speaking to him about the letter he wrote, he tells me that when I get out of prison, he is going to beat me in Madden 2010 (the Play Station football video game).

Of course, I tell him that he will not win but he pleads his case about using special codes that I don't know about. It feels great just hearing the confidence that he has. We end our phone call with I love yous.

October 2009 – I find out that my son is obsessed with having a six pack (abdominal muscles). His mother tells me that my son is constantly lifting his shirt up every time he walks by her full-size mirror. All I can say to her is, like father, like son and I encourage him to eat right and exercise. There is a serious problem in today's society with obesity, especially with kids. So, I believe that it's good that he wants to have a cut-up stomach. My son gets on the phone and asks me if I have a six pack and I tell him that it's almost there but I'm not satisfied with it yet. He tells me that he has a 2 pack and his mom tells him there's no such thing, so of course, I have to explain it to him the best way

I can without undermining **what she** tells him. I tell him I will help him with his **six pack w**hen I get home and that he should keep doing **his exerc**ises and eating more fruits and vegetables. **He replies** that he loves and misses me until infinit**y, which** is his favorite word.

October 31, 2009 – Hallowe**en and I** don't know what my son is going to be becaus**e I don't h**ave minutes to call him. Nor has he or his **mother wr**itten me to tell me what he wants to be. It'**s okay bec**ause I will call him tomorrow, on the 1st of **November** to find out.

November 1, 2009 – I speak **to my son** and he is very excited to hear my voice. H**is mother** tells me about a field trip that my son wen**t on, to** the apple farm. I was told that my son was **throwing** apples at the other kid's feet and running **up and** down the aisles.

Of course, he said it wasn't him, so the teacher sent a letter home stating that my son must have an adult accompany him on all other trips. It's very important that I get home to raise my son with tough love, so he doesn't stay off track. He is a good kid that needs his father's guidance. His mother also tells me that he received a good letter from school the next week after that occasion at the farm. He has been conducting himself with respect for himself and his peers. That's my boy. I love him when he messes up and I love him when he does good.

November 2, 2009 – I received a letter from my beautiful mother today and she expressed how much she missed me. She also let me know how she felt about me as a man of courage and valor, telling me to get all I can so I can be prepared for new challenges. She lets me know that my son told her, he truly misses his daddy!! The ministry that I belong to is very excited and very anxious for me to come home. It feels good to be missed and cared about. It motivates me to stay focused and learn all that I can so that I can be 10x better than I once was. I want to be spiritually, mentally, physically, emotionally and financially complete. I will know that there's always room for improvement.

November 11, 2009 – I call my son and to my surprise, he is excited to hear my voice and I'm just as excited to hear his. He tells me about his test scores from school that he keeps for me. As he tells me how good he's doing in school, I can feel his excitement for learning. So, I continue to encourage him to gain all the knowledge he can and have fun doing it. I explain to my 8-year-old son that knowledge is power and no one can take that away from him. I tell him to keep up the good work and asked him what he wants for his birthday, which is December 2nd. He tells me that he wants an I-pod and a new DS game but one of them could be for Christmas. That response lets me know that my son is learning to be considerate of my current financial situation. My son is used to getting anything from his dad, especially when he deserves it. I feel good inside today, knowing that my son is showing good signs of growth. I'm so ready to get home and continue raising my boy to become a great man.

November 26, 2009 – Thanksgiving Day and I am still incarcerated at MDC Brooklyn. I truly believed that I would be home with my family by now, but that's not the case. It makes me wonder about this journey that I'm currently on. Somewhere in my past, I must have done quite a few things wrong to encounter this trial and tribulation, and trust me, it hurts to the core. I choose to turn all feelings off to everything and everyone that mean something to me! I'm tired of hurting and it's not fair to put those that love me through the same pain and agony that I'm feeling. I'm better off being numb for the rest of my time here in prison. I decide not to call home today and just let my family enjoy themselves. I continue to pray for my loved ones and those who tried to help me stay positive through these difficult times.

November 30, 2009 – It's Monday and I've made it through the Thanksgiving holiday. Thank God for football being available to me on the TV. It helps to temporarily keep my mind off my family. I am feeling a bit down today as I prepare to go to work, so I find myself getting emotional about wanting to hug my son. I've felt this way before but today seems a bit overwhelming and I believe it's because his birthday is coming up on December 2nd. Everything that could get me upset seems to be getting under my skin when normally I would be able to dismiss any negative vibes. I assume that I'm at a boiling point and I need to release these emotions before it turns ugly. My faith in God is still going strong and I realize that it's okay to let it out by crying. I cry and it feels very good to know that even in a place such as this, God still gives me a comfort zone to embrace but most of all, I could be understood all the same!

VISIONARY!!

CHAPTER 4

THE GAME OF FOOTBALL

I already shared with you how I got involved in playing the game of football. Now, I can explain to you what football means to me and how it pertains to every aspect of my life.

Football is unlike any other sport. While it has similar principles with other games, namely being responsible and dedicated, it teaches you life skills that you cannot learn off the field. For example, it taught me that your teammates' success is your success too.

There is a particular focus involved that places you in a zone. True athletes know that when you are in this zone, your mind is sharper, your spirit doesn't allow much to bother you, your soul is not easily broken and your body feels like a superhero.

The game of football has required from me a very disciplined workout and eating regimen. Although there is a high risk of getting physically hurt you do not have longevity in this game without a physical awareness. Lifting weights, functional exercises, dynamic stretching and water therapy are a must to maintain the physical endurance necessary to play the game.

All these things require the proper preparation for your body and muscles to recover as soon as possible after a game.

In preparing for a season, the team would go through a training camp scenario. We would practice twice a day for three-hour sessions (each practice). We would do running, sprints, football drills and then more running. After either session, we would do weight training. The weight training was done as a team during camp. During the football season, players did individual weight training. It was easy to see who took their training seriously by how well they performed.

It's vital to eat good carbohydrates before games to maintain your energy level. Carbohydrates help athletes produce energy. Healthy fats, vegetables and mainly protein aid in muscle recovery.

Although people view football as a violent and brutal sport, there is a lot more to it. Football is a way of life. It is a parallel to life. You have your ups and your downs. You take a risk, but you have to keep living. In life, you risk the chance of getting into a car accident or something else happening to you. You have to live; you have to go to work. In the sport, you make that choice. There are so many variables that can affect what happens to you. Your foot can get caught in the turf, you can have a bad collision with another player or your ankle or knee can give out. You physically push your body to its ultimate limit. When you think you cannot take that next step you reach deep into your soul and push yourself for that extra yard. Those are the risks you take in playing the game.

There is a beauty to the game that a lot of people don't understand. The game has taught a lot of people how to be decent human beings. How to love, how to care for others, how to channel certain energy and use it as a positive experience. Football is bigger than just X's and O's lining up on the field and running plays. The parallel to life is so much greater than any other sport. The game has taught me how to become stronger and to never quit. It has kept me focused on goals each month and year. Giving your all to something that you are passionate about allows you to grow. Having that passion and talent that you know was God-given teaches you how to put things into perspective and focus on your grind and learn from your mistakes. Falling and getting back up is the only way to achieve your goal. In playing football, just as in life, you are going to fall. You get back up and you do it a little bit differently the next time, to obtain a different result. It makes you analyze what you did wrong and learn from it.

Life, just like football, presents similar challenges and choices. The game of football touches everyone who is involved in it; the players, fans, coaches, and owners. It is a camaraderie, despite its main purpose of competition.

The components of football make up a family that support each other in every way. Your friends, parents, kids, spouse, whoever, cheers for you and your team. They believe in your purpose and your reason for playing the game. They want you to succeed. We learn, we grow, we teach. In the game, you must be teachable and eventually teach. You must be able to stay focused, to give and sacrifice for the betterment of the team. In life, there are so many sacrifices for you to become successful.

Football has taught me so much about life. For example, friendships and brotherhood are built with your teammates that are unbreakable. You go through the fire with your team, but you don't let the opposition break that bond. **That's wh**at the game of football has built in a lot of **young me**n and women that are playing the game.

As I was coming up in hi**gh school,** my best friend, Sha-meil Simpkins and I ha**d a thing** that we would do on game day. I played the **fullback** position and he was a tailback. Every home **game, we** would go out to the 50-yard line on the **football** field. We would wrestle with each other to see **who was** the strongest. After this we stretched, pra**yed and** fought, getting ourselves psyched up and re**ady for the** game. To this day I am currently the win**ner. In t**elling you this story, Sha-meil is going to re**ad this and** say that's not how it was. That was our th**ing, that** kept us bonded. We protected each other o**n the foot**ball field and that is something I have alw**ays held d**ear to my heart because it meant a lot to bo**th of us.** To this day, we can walk up to each other and do the same thing. We felt it in our hearts to build that relationship, just as you create relationships in life through work, school, family or your place of worship.

The game of football has truly been a blessing to me in different ways and I have so many stories I can tell.

In May of 1995, months before Delaware State's football camp started, my colleague, Ray Bias and I, took on a job that the coach got us. We worked for a trucking company. It was really hot that summer. We were picking up pianos, old Jacuzzis and such from people's houses. We agreed with one another that the job was a bit too much as it was too hot and required a lot of manual labor. One day we were loading the truck up and a refrigerator fell on me. I looked at BJ and he looked at me. I dropped the refrigerator, stood it up and I walked off the job. We went back to the apartment, cooked some food, relaxed, talked and laughed about that job and that experience. Coach Collick had set us up. He knew that was going to be some serious work and that's why he got us that job. I tell that story because the relationships I've built with my colleagues and teammates will last a lifetime. The hard work that we had to put in, the fellowship we created and taking care of each other was worth everything that we were put through. The relationship we now have is priceless.

Here is another story that means so much to me because of the relationship that was established with one of my teammates.

When I transferred to Delaware State I met someone who I truly consider as my brother, Burt

Watson. He took me under his wing as a fullback that time. I couldn't play when I came in, but I could practice so we would work out together. He would show me things from the fullback perspective. He passed the torch down to me, but we created an unbreakable bond and relationship. There was one day that I would never forget. It was during Delaware State's homecoming. I was living in Virginia and I came up to Maryland to meet Burt and we rode to Delaware together. We didn't plan on staying, so we headed back to Baltimore after we spent the day in Delaware. We were very tired and Burt was driving. It was so foggy that we didn't know where we were and ended up right in front of the ocean. We could have driven right into the water. When Burt woke me up, I looked around, shook my head, glanced at him and went right back to sleep. We laughed because it was no one but God that spared us from tragedy.

What I'm trying to say in all of this is that I never felt like I was in danger being with him. Our strong relationship made me feel secure and allowed me to trust him. We made our way out of there and back to his house. We talk about that incident year after year. We know that God kept us from going into the water. Our relationship has always gotten stronger. You meet people for a reason. You build certain relationships because of the game of football. This game has created so many positive outcomes and results in my life. Relationships that go for years and years. It creates moments in your life that you will never forget and you will hold dear to your heart. It is so much bigger than wins and losses. I've learned that throughout my years.

Everywhere I have gone, I created relationships with people that have shown me love. When brothers can show each other love in this way it is powerful. The game of football is responsible for creating a lot of great things in this world and in my life. It constantly reminds me that you never need easy, you just need possible. When you are faced with those moments in life when you are not the prettiest, you are not the smartest, or you are not the best, focus on something that motivates you like the game of football has motivated me.

CHAPTER 5

STAYING FOCUSED

Accepting and condoning self-growth means being willing to learn more, seeing things without blinders or through a different glass, and finding a way to open your eyes wider than ever before to achieve more, because there's always another level of your greatness.

Sometimes in life, it is easy to get caught up. We have schedules and lives that can be absorbed by our circumstances. What I have learned through my experiences is that, sometimes, those who we surround ourselves with the most can often cloud our vision and block us from truly seeing the beauty of this thing we call life. My journey has been long and challenging and it has taken me to this point. I am grateful for the strength provided to me by a greater power. He has supplied me with the courage to keep going even when I thought I couldn't take another step.

Most times, when people look at me, they see a man with one eye. Those who know me, however, understand that I am a man that sees more clearly than most, even with one eye. And I mean that physically and figuratively. The loss of my eye, the challenges I have faced and most of all, my faith in

God have given me a clarity to endure and overcome numerous obstacles.

Many have asked severally, how I did all of this and to me, that is the best question of them all. Life's journey has taken me to many places through different trials and tribulations. These trials and tribulations have allowed me to learn and awaken my inner self, my inner being, my spirit man. When you are awakened, your eyes open. You address things differently. You see things differently. You no longer see them in the ways of a young boy or girl. You no longer see things one way. There are dimensions to it. I finally opened my eyes to a lot of things that could hold me back from reaching my goals and aspirations.

I wonder how many of you are being held back for the same reason because your eyes were closed. Your spirit man was shut off; it was numb to what you were doing. I want to instill in you that when you awaken that spirit man inside you, the warrior inside you, you will see things differently. Your eyes will be opened, and you will see clearly. You will see the end of the tunnel and you will discover your purpose. You will see and feel your situation changing. Only then can you move to the next step or the next level. Never allow yourself to be held back again.

Once your eyes are open, take advantage of your new self because you will be able to attain more. You will go after everything you want with a different energy. You will know your purpose. This enlightenment you will receive is a gradual process, you can't get it all in one shot because you are not perfect. God did not make us perfect, but He did make us in his image so that we can strive to be perfect.

There are different levels of awakening and becoming aware. Never stop understanding that the levels are constantly changing, depending on the current situation in your life.

Never shut off your opportunity to grow by thinking you have all the answers. I always challenge people to try to do better and try to reach deep within themselves and know that there are levels of its growth. There is always another level so always look to open your eyes.

It is easy to get sidetracked in life. I have learned how important it is to stay grounded. In my life, meditation is something that I use to help me stay grounded. This practice was recommended to me by someone that I admire, and it was a game changer for me. Meditation is a time when I can be quiet and reflect.

There are some principles that I believe can help anyone in their journey. These are things that I employ in my thinking almost every day. It helps me to continue to develop myself, open my eyes to new concepts and stay focused on my goal.

Self-awareness

Merriam-Webster's dictionary defines self-awareness as an awareness of one's own personality or individuality.

In order to get anywhere you want to go, you must first be very self-aware of where you are in your struggle, your goal or your situation. For example, if you are struggling with a specific area in your life, being self-aware of the problem will allow you to work on it to improve your situation and bring you closer to where you want to be. Be aware of your actions.

Understand that you are responsible for the things you do and their consequences. The problem may be with something you are doing yourself, not an external factor. Sometimes we block our own progress by not opening our mind to different alternatives and options. Being self-aware in your goals, desires and motivations will help you to overcome obstacles that you create yourself.

Surround yourself with winners

"Surround yourself with the dreamers and the doers, the believers and thinkers, but most of all, surround yourself with those who see the greatness within in you, even when you don't see it yourself." Edmund Lee, author.

You must surround yourself with people that are positive and understand your goals, dreams or problems. Even if they don't agree with something you decide, people who lift you up will always be in your corner to support you mentally and emotionally. They will give you constructive criticism and the energy to continue to believe in your purpose.

Most times the toxic people in our lives are family members, church members, co-workers and close friends because they are the people we are around the most. It doesn't matter if you see them every day. If they are detrimental to your progress and positive being, you must remove them from your life or greatly diminish the interaction you have with them. If they are not adding value to your life, make a choice. Time is valuable so choose wisely. We unconsciously become like the people we are around. Ask yourself if you would want to trade places with that person. *Are they in a position in life that would be beneficial to me?*

I always try to surround myself with those who will elevate my thinking and energy. I do not have time to let people drag me down with negativity and lack of progress in their own lives. I take my inspiration from those who want to succeed, not those who are complacent with accepting their situations. We all face bad situations in life, but I need people in my life who search for an alternative or solution to better themselves and create different opportunities. Building relationships that last a lifetime helps you to navigate through life.

One of my best friends, and a man I call my brother, Amare Terrell, always believed in me, even when we were young and playing little league football. He always found a way to keep me inspired and looked after me. He constantly gave me a positive word and true word. If things weren't right, he would let me know. Our relationship has grown over the years and we are at the point today where we are doing business together. Even in our business ventures, his work ethic has taught me how to continue to work hard and to continue to believe in my dreams and move forward with vigor, passion, and energy. He taught me how to market and advertise any product that you want people to know about or purchase. After watching him all these years, I mirror a lot of his technique because he understands the consumer.

I will continue to tell people that if you find friends that you can build and grow with and that will not always tell you yes and can tell you no when you need to hear it, keep them by your side. This journey that we call life has its ups and downs but it's always good to have someone on your side and someone you can talk to. For me, in this book, it's all about me building relationships with my colleagues, my friends I grew up with, my coaches and my mentors. This is how I was able to make it through this far. I will continue to need those people in my life and vice versa. When you can find true friendship, it's worth holding on to. And always giving them love and support, that's what it's all about.

If you want to move forward with your dreams, goals, or career, I highly recommend that you take a step toward changing your environment by evaluating the core group that surrounds you.

Faith

> *"Now faith is the substance of things hoped for, the evidence of things not seen."* **(King James Version, Hebrews 11:1)**

We all need something to lift us, to remind us that God doesn't make mistakes. Whoever your God is, be sure to stay grounded in your beliefs of a higher power.

Spiritual belief will lift you to greater heights. My faith in God has gotten me through the toughest times in my life. Trusting and believing in Him has made me understand that it is not me that controls my fate. I am the man that must facilitate and execute all aspects of my life; my business, my family, my marriage, and myself. I make the choices in life that can affect me positively or negatively but if I want the success that I strive for, I must believe that God has the ultimate choice and decision for what happens.

Keeping myself in prayer on a regular basis and attending my church services keeps me grounded and aware that my faith affects everything I do.

*"Yet what we suffer now **is nothing** compared to the glory He will reveal **to us later."** (**New Living Translation, Romans 8:18**)*

Gratitude

They say that gratitude **truly chang**es everything. In my experience, that has **been the t**otal truth. You may not be exactly where **you want** to be or have exactly what you want at th**is moment** but if you can focus on what you have rig**ht now and** be grateful, it will allow more to flow into **your life.**

Gratitude makes us who **we are. It** can boost your career or goals, improve pe**rsonal rel**ationships and marriages and improve you**r attitude.** There are so many benefits to being gr**ateful and** there is even evidence to show that it can **improve** our health.

I believe in being thankful because you never know what twists and turns life has for us. You can choose to be down and out about your situation, but you must remember that there is always someone who has it much worse than you do. I am so grateful for what I have experienced and what I have gone through because it has established relationships in my life that positively affect me every day. It helps me in my faith to understand that God chooses what we have and don't have. He has molded my entire life, so I will take the bad with the good because I know there is much more to come.

I am grateful for the game of football because of the experience and discipline it gave me, the physical stamina and mental agility and the bonds and relationships that were created throughout my football career.

Staying Focused

Being blinded to all the things that can hold you back or distract you from your goals is much more challenging than you might imagine. Remember this, you just don't wake up strong and, as I've written earlier, you never need easy, you just need possible. When you are weighed down by life's challenges, remember your purpose and your vision.

I have had some challenging periods of my life where I could have easily decided to give up. When I felt this way, I took a step back and prepared to do the following things.

First off, I took time to be alone. I found that one does their best thinking alone. I would sit quietly and reflect, allowing myself to feel the pain, despair, disappointment. It is okay to feel all these things. It is normal, but I never let myself get stuck in this place for too long. I acknowledged these feelings and then moved on.

Secondly, I would make a list of all the things I wanted, why I wanted them and how I would get them (you can write it down or say it out loud). Next, I took small steps towards getting the things that I had listed. And, even though obstacles came during these steps, I just kept going. One of the most important things that I did was giving to others in *my* time of need. Acts of kindness really go a long way.

You see, we are all people no matter what color, creed, religion or sexual preference. At the end of the day, we all want the same things: love, respect, appreciation, and acknowledgment. You won't believe how much a sincere compliment through text, a phone call or in person given to someone can change everything... I dare you to try it and see for yourself.

Finally, I created a vision board. This is something that you can look at every day to remind yourself of your goals. I had a list of things I wanted to accomplish and then the date when they were finished or established. I also cut out some pictures of things that were inspirational to me. You can set up your board any way that works for you but have it in a place where it is easily accessible, so you can update it as you see fit.

You just don't wake up strong. Opposition, adversity, and the challenges in your life help determine your strength level. You just don't wake up strong. The things that we go through in life challenge our mind, our spirits, and our bodies. That's what makes us stronger each day. You have to find time to edify the mind, body, and soul so they grow and get stronger.

This will enable you to deal with opposition, obstacles, and adversity.

There have been plenty of challenges in my life. I've been through different things that have almost broken me down and made me want to quit, but that was not an option. When you tell yourself that you want success, you want to be greater than something that's greater than you. When you yearn for something that's greater than you, quitting is not an option. No one said it would be easy. If it was easy, everybody would be doing it. I find in life that it's not what you go through, it's *how* you go through what you're going through that determines what kind of person you want to become. Each day you're going to go through something that will challenge your mind, challenge your body and your soul and you must find it deep within yourself to fight through it. You have to make it to the other side. Once you get on that other side, you will feel exuberant. You will feel uplifted, empowered, inspired and motivated because you've beaten the opposition.

You just don't wake up strong. Challenges are there to test you and make you a better person. In my life, my ability to get through the adversity that I faced, and the obstacles that I overcame was through God. My strength comes from God; having that faith to know that He's going to get me through it. They say faith without works is dead so, at the end of the day, you still have to put one foot in front of the other. You have to push through and believe that God will guide you and help you get through it every step of the way. They say you just have to have faith the size of a mustard seed. That's all you to make it.

Had I not followed the plan that God gave me, I wouldn't be where I am today. Persistence is key. Find the inner strength to keep pushing. Never give up. That's how life is. You have to be committed to whatever you want to do. It still isn't easy. I have to grind every day to make things happen. And tomorrow, there may be a different opposition, but you have to have faith and lean on God, trusting that He will bring you through it.

I've been overcoming obstacles all my life: two years old with a tumor in my left eye, a prosthetic eye, a lifelong disability. I've been fighting all my life so why would I lay down now, because I'm facing another obstacle, another opposition, more adversity.

Keep fighting. Keep going. Never give up. If you get knocked down, get back up. That increase of strength will give you endurance. You just didn't wake up strong. This is what life is about. You have God on your side, but you have to put the work in. You will receive nothing if you don't put the work in. You sow those seeds, you plant those seeds, you water those seeds, and before you know it, your harvest is here.

CHAPTER 6

THE END IS THE BEGINNING

The end of this book is really the beginning of the rest of my story. There are so many things that are in the plans for my life and my business, but I needed to tell my story, share my knowledge and hopefully inspire those who need some guidance and hope.

As I mentioned before, alkaline water is the newest aspect of my brand. I was fortunate enough to be introduced to the team of a water company, Alka

Warrior Water. The blessing in this is that the blueprint of the Fabian Thorne Built2Last involves nutrition. In the process of building one's body through physical fitness, nutrition plays a major part. This water is an alkaline water that hydrates your body on a cellular level and increases your energy level. It has all-natural electrolytes. The water has been heated to a certain temperature to cause a reverse osmosis process which cleans the water and brings it to a certain level of alkalinity. In learning so much about how this water hydrates you, cleanses your skin, lubricates your joints and detoxifies your body, it was a no-brainer for me. Built2Last and Alka Warrior combined forces to create a movement. When I talk about mind, body, and soul in relation to my brand, I now have a new level of my business that is introduced through physical fitness, nutritional guidance and motivational speaking. In order for people to find out about how good this water tastes and how good the nutritional component is, marketing and advertising are key.

The Alka Warrior and Fabian Thorne Built2Last brands have been working together for over a year and a half now. We have been building each other up, spreading and sharing the healthy components of alkaline water. One important thing to know about alkaline water is that by putting your body in an alkaline state, certain diseases cannot survive in this environment. The importance of the water is to build and maintain your health by hydrating on a cellular level. According to a study by H.H. Mitchell published in *the Journal of Biological Chemistry*, an adult human body can be up to 60% water. The brain and the heart are 73% water and the lungs are about 83% water. The muscles and kidneys are 79% water, the skin is 64% and the bones are 31%. Knowing that water is the major component of your body, you want to put the best water in your body. A lot of bottles used for water have chemicals such as BPA. Alka Warrior uses BPA-free bottles with a shelf life of two years. We are conscious about how we bottle our water, we are conscious of what's in our water and we want people to get exactly what they need out of our water.

To elaborate a little bit more on the end being the beginning, I will tell you about the different entities of the Built2last brand and how they are moving forward. The apparel line will have its own production facility to fully equip the fitness industry. The apparel line will also be displayed by our own fitness models. This book will generate a book tour to accompany the motivational speaking in colleges. The fitness entity is working on having its own state-of-the-art facility with an indoor turf field, indoor pool, steam room, sauna, and video room. We will be able to educate our athletes on speed, agility, flexibility, and power and show them how to maximize on all of these facets. The facility will host NFL combines, high school combines, football camps, speed and agility camps for all sports. We will not just be limited to football because all sports deal with speed, agility, and power.

The fitness company will be launching its own line of supplements, such as proteins, fat burners, and branch chain amino acids. The training facility will have a juice bar that offers healthy wraps, shakes and other food items, as well as all of our supplements. These are some of the things that the Built2last brand will be introducing in 2018.

I will reiterate that building relationships has allowed the Fabian Thorne Built2last brand to evolve. Those strong relationships, with mentors, colleagues, and clients has allowed me to navigate and take the brand to new levels. It is so important that we build strong, positive connections in order to be successful. Learning from those relationships will allow you to minimize your mistakes and maximize your results. The importance of these connections is to sharpen each other, bring something to the table that is of quality, that has substance and will always help enhance those relationships. The Fabian Thorne Built2last brand is built on this concept. I believe in my relationships because of the hard work, blood, sweat, and tears that has been put into them. The passion of what you believe in is what drives those bonds to new levels. This is how we have been successful and that's how we will continue to be successful.

In the Fabian Thorne Built2Last brand, through its evolution and current timeline, God has shown me that my diligence and perseverance is paying off. Working hard and working smart is opening new doors for me and my business. I've never met a successful person that hasn't gone through failures or challenges and obstacles. In this evolution of Fabian Thorne Built2Last, having my team, my developing apparel line, my motivational speaking, and this book, You Just Don't Wake Up Strong are all a dream come true for me. The best is yet to come with a fitness center, a private training facility and any other upcoming facets that will move my company forward. The bible says that faith without work is dead (James 2:14). I've always had the faith and I 've always had the desire to work hard, train and work for what I believe in.

I'm excited about where I am at today and where I am going. I appreciate everyone that is reading this book. I appreciate all those who have supported me and Built2Last over the years through this journey. You will always get more and more from me and from my brand. You will never be disappointed, and I will always provide quality, whether it is through my motivational speaking, the apparel line, my training and even my acting roles. My success will be based on my foundation, my team who bring everything together and make it all work. If you don't have the right team in place, you will not be able to move forward and build your brand. You must have those that don't just see the money but see your vision and believe in it. This is what the Fabian Thorne Built2Last evolution is all about. Onward and upward!

QUOTES

"My dad is not just my dad he's also my coach. He guided me through thick and thin. We will always continue to have a strong relationship. He tries his best to keep me happy through the good and bad. That's why I will always love and cherish him."

Fabian Thorne Jr, son, age 17

"I think that my dad is kind and helpful. He is funny and sweet and also busy. I miss him when he is not home, but I appreciate

all he does for me. I love my dad very, very much."

Jayda Thorne, daughter, age 7

Being married to Fabian Thorne for almost 12 years has taught me a lot about him, but the qualities that I admire the most in him are his positivity and his perseverance. I could not have gotten through these years without his faith, love and endless desire to go onward and upward. If I ever feel down or feel like giving up, I look to him for strength. Thanks for being my rock all these years my love!"

Anna K. Thorne, wife

"Those who know my son, Fabian Thorne, know that he played the game of football from age 7 to 37. Football was his passion...you would think he was born with a football in his hands. Although he had a certain obstacle against him, he never gave in to it. He actually became quite successful. He is now CEO of his own company, FT Built2Last. I'm very proud of how he has always endeavored to reach and accomplish higher levels of success in life. He has such an impeccable and strong drive for bigger and better. Fabian has really made me glad he is my son!!! Better yet, I'm glad he is a God-Fearing man...dwelling under the shadow

of the Almighty and that gives me joy unspeakable!"

Annie Thorne, mother

"To be the brother of Fabian Thorne aka Bear has been a remarkable experience and a very interesting journey. Ever since I was a little boy, I kept my eyes on him. I always found myself completely amazed at how he would overcome any and every obstacle that came his way. My brother and I are like night and day. I realized that his tough love was only because he wanted me to be the best man I could be...strong, tough and able to hold my own. That is something he instilled in me and I am grateful for it. As time passed

by and we matured into young men, I noticed incredible characteristics that he possessed...bravery, courage, intelligence at a high level and most importantly, his willpower to always strive to be the best!"

Chad Thorne, brother

"My cousin, Fabian, better known as Bear, has played a major role in my life since childhood. He was definitely a role model to me back then and still is to this day. Growing up in the inner city of East Orange, NJ wasn't the easiest thing to do, but in my eyes, Bear made it look easy. He was well respected in the community, he loved his family, always remained an honor roll student in school, and was one of the best athletes in

the state! Me coming up a few years behind him, made me want to follow his exact footsteps! When the average person meets Fabian their first reaction is, I see how he got that name...looking at his muscle-bound and stocky stature, you immediately think of a bear. With knowing Bear all my life, my description of his nickname is a little different from the average. Fabian is very protective of his family and relentless like a bear, and whatever he puts his mind to he attacks it like a bear!"

Walter Holloway, cousin

"The Fabian that played running back for me at Trinity College was a smart, hard-nosed football player with a big heart.

*Opposing teams hated **to try a**nd tackle Fabian because he ran **so hard the**y thought they would get hurt **ta**c**kling him**. Off the field, Fabian was a big-**hearted** fun-loving guy who his teammates **and coach**es enjoyed being around. You cou**ld see the** influence of Fabian's mother on **his life and** the way he treated people with **respect and** dignity. He loved his mom an**d never w**anted to do anything to cause he**r pain.** You would never know he grew up i**n one of the** toughest areas of New Jersey. I'm **very blessed** to have coached a young man **like Fabian** Thorne."*

Leslie Frazier,

Buffalo Bills Defensive

Coordinator / **mentor**

"My fan, my hero. The inner peace I feel as I watch Fabian educate and teach his craft is my reward. So thankful to have enlightened him to bring out his ability".

Lawrence Athill, coach/mentor

"My brother, Fabian Thorne, inspires me with his resiliency to overcome odds, his constant pursuit of greatness. His unwillingness to help others achieve their goals in life. A true friend is someone who wants the best for them as well as others around you."

Amare Terrell, entrepreneur / best friend

"Since I met Fabian on the first day of kindergarten, he has continued to be one of the most inspirational people I've met. His tenacious drive and pursuit of excellence has always set him apart. Our hometown hero continues to break down barriers and set new standards."

Tabari Sturdavent, childhood friend

"Ignoring what many would consider a disability or, at best, a limitation, Fabian Thorne soldiered on to a successful professional sports career. His life is a testament to the fact that strength - physical, emotional, moral,

and spiritual - results from a committed lifestyle. 'You Just Don't Wake Up' Strong does not derive from scholarly research ... but from his committed life."

Reginald A. Jennings,
mentor / business advisor

""Big Bear" inspired me since our youth. His grit, determination, and spirit are unmatched in past or future days. He's a born winner no matter the circumstance and a man that I've always preferred on my team even [though] it didn't always seem that way. Bear is a fearless [and] tireless competitor whether on the basketball court, football field, or at the kitchen table! I've known Bear for many

years and not once did he use his eye as an "excuse" or "disability". If not for him sharing his life's journey on the radio or social media these days, I would never in a trillion years consider this "machine" disabled in any way. Neither would the helpless linebackers that couldn't tackle him, nor the centers that tried to block his shot. I've been fortunate and Blessed to count him as a brother, friend, teammate, mentor, competitor, confidante, and servant throughout the years".

Rick Butler, childhood friend

"Fabian inspires me through his authentic approach... everything he does is real. He's a true leader in the urban community for

*the youth and the older adults. He has
helped me along my journey and has also
been a mentor and a big brother. Fabian
is a hustler and a true advocate on how to
make something out of nothing."*

**Elijah Shumate,
professional football player / client**

*"Fabian Thorne changed my life. Growing
up, I always struggled with fitness and
mental happiness. Fabian took my life
and turned me into a fit, go-getter. Now,
I believe I can do anything. Fabian will
always be a mentor to me".*

Brendan Jackson, client / mentee

"Fabian Thorne is an **awesome** man of God whom I truly beli**eve has be**en gifted to inspire, motivate **and** encourage a generation. His love of **health and** wellness and his passion for hel**ping other**s achieve their personal fitness g**oals is par**t of what makes him one of the best **at what** he does!"

Faith Davina, Team Built2Last

"For me, I always wa**nt to be a** man of integrity and stick to m**y word. I am** always on a mission to surro**und myself** not only with the best in the ind**ustry but** the best of humankind. When I m**et Fabian** Thorne, he exuded both of these **qualities.** I am proud to call him my f**riend. In** keeping to the point, positive and **focused,** this is all

I have to say about his story. The best is yet to come."

Johnny Salami,

business owner / business partner

"What can I say about Fabian Thorne... This is a guy who inspires me every day to get it done! He is a guy who has overcome so many adversities in his life, yet never once has been controlled by them. I can refer to him as a beast on the battlefield of life. This guy pushes through with strength in everything he does. He is a very humble and Godly man, a great father, and a great son. As an owner of Alka Warrior, I am beyond proud to have this guy on my team. The

name Built2Last is the perfect title for this guy, for he is a warrior or life."

Lou Ravennati,

business owner / business partner

"Fabian's character exemplifies persistence, honor, and dedication to goals. Throughout his life, he has always worked towards becoming a better version of himself and he shares that vision with his clients in his training methods. Fabian leads by example; teaching his clients to compete to become better versions of themselves. I am honored to count him among my friends."

Shari Spivek, Team Built2Last

"Did you ever cross someone's path and just know there was something magical about them? Well, this is exactly how I felt when I met Fabian Thorne. Fabian has guided my life in ways I could never have imagined. Fabian is a true leader, inspiring, a giver and just an amazing person who lives his life always paying it forward. I feel blessed to call him my friend."

Rae Lyn Ciccone, friend

"When I think about Fabian "Bear" Thorne, I think about perseverance. Over the years, Fabian has shown his resilience and his drive to overcome ALL obstacles. As an athlete, Fabian embraced the expected work ethic, as an entrepreneur, Fabian is enthusiastic,

and as a brother, he values quality time for his family and friends. I have never been surprised by his accomplishments. He engenders the qualities of a true pioneer. Fabian has accepted his faults, shortcomings, and mistakes. I don't know many people like him; he is one of a kind."

Derek Cradle, Educator

"Fabian's strong desire to succeed is infectious. He continuously challenges himself in order to grow every day into the best version of himself he can be. His will to win motivates his clients to also step up and challenge themselves."

Natasha Blair, Team Built2Last

"Fabian has always displayed an incredible work ethic for pushing and motivating others towards greatness! He has an unquestionable belief that no obstacle is too great to overcome, nor any dream is too big to obtain. I am not surprised at the man, husband, father and friend that he is but I am thankful that today he is sharing himself with the world. I am forever honored to know you and to have you as a friend...Keep grinding!"

Keith Jarvis, Friend / Business Partner

"Fabian strives to be more than successful, he strives to be of value! He has inspired many including myself to live our dreams

*and not our fears. He is **the true** definition of a blessing and of a **friend."***

Rashelle Williams, Investor / friend

*"Fabian is a brother th**at I have** known for over 30 years. He has a**lways had** the spirit and the drive to not be **denied on** any level he chooses to succeed. **He has in**spired me to step up and I am th**ankful** God placed him in my life."*

Rhashawn Knox Investor / childhood friend

*"Fabian is the most **dynamic** individual I know. He is a force t**o be recko**ned with and well recognized. **One of my** favorite*

things about Fabian is his superpower of faith that gives glory to God. His energy is a catalyst that makes a powerful impact, way beyond the gym."

Thasheena Cunto, Director of Strategic Initiatives Team Built2Last

ACKNOWLEDGMENTS

First and foremost, I would like to thank God for His divine protection and unwavering love. I would not be here today if it weren't for His grace, mercy, and favor. I love you and I am forever grateful my Lord. Thank you!

To my wife and kids, you are one of the main reasons I grind so hard. The love and support from you have played a major role in my quest to become a better man.

To my family, my mom, siblings and host of cousins and friends, I carry a piece of you all with me daily to remind me of the love we all share.

To my leader, my pastor, and friend, there is so much I could say about your loyalty, love, dedication, spiritual guidance, and caring ways, but that would be another book!

To my church family, thank you for the prayers and laughter that we have shared throughout the years. God bless you all.

To my Built2Last team, I want to thank you all for your continuing loyalty and dedication throughout the years. I am grateful for you all embracing the vision that God gave me.

Team Alka Warrior, I'm forever grateful for you guys believing in the Fabian Thorne Built2Last brand. I am excited about what we, as partners, team Alka

Warrior and team Built 2 Last will create in the near future and beyond.

To every coach and mentor, I want to thank you for being such positive role models in my life.

CPSIA information can be obtained
at www.ICGtesting.com
Printed in the USA
FSHW021909050519
57864FS

9 781949 169591